Owlkids Books Inc.
10 Lower Spadina Avenue, Suite 400, Toronto, Ontario M5V 2Z2
www.owlkidsbooks.com

North America edition © 2013 Owlkids Books Inc.
Translation © 2012 Sarah Quinn

Published in France under the title *Une journée à la ferme* © 2012
Éditions Escabelle, 33 rue d'Aboukir, 75002 Paris

Distributed in Canada by University of Toronto Press
5201 Dufferin Street, Toronto, Ontario M3H 5T8

Distributed in the United States by Publishers Group West
1700 Fourth Street, Berkeley, California 94710

Library and Archives Canada Cataloguing in Publication

Cordier, Séverine
    A day at the farm / created by Séverine Cordier and Cynthia Lacroix.

Translation of: Une journée à la ferme.
ISBN 978-1-926973-76-0

    1. Vocabulary--Juvenile literature. 2. Word recognition--Juvenile
literature. I. Lacroix, Cynthia II. Title.

PE1449.C66 2013   j428.1   C2012-904868-2

Library of Congress Control Number: 2012948721

Design: lacroixdesign.fr

Canadian Heritage	Patrimoine canadien	Canadä	Ontario — Ontario Media Development Corporation / Société de développement de l'industrie des médias de l'Ontario
Canada Council for the Arts	Conseil des Arts du Canada	ONTARIO ARTS COUNCIL / CONSEIL DES ARTS DE L'ONTARIO	

We acknowledge the financial support of the Canada Council for the Arts, the Ontario Arts Council, the
Government of Canada through the Canada Book Fund (CBF) and the Government of Ontario through
the Ontario Media Development Corporation's Book Initiative for our publishing activities.

Manufactured by Toppan Leefung Packaging & Printing (Dongguan) Co., Ltd.
Manufactured in Dongguan, China, in October 2012
Job #BAYDC1

A   B   C   D   E   F

Publisher of Chirp, chickaDEE and OWL
www.owlkidsbooks.com

A Day at the Farm

SÉVERINE CORDIER • CYNTHIA LACROIX

Owl kids

jacket

boots

"Let's go!"

"Are we there yet?"

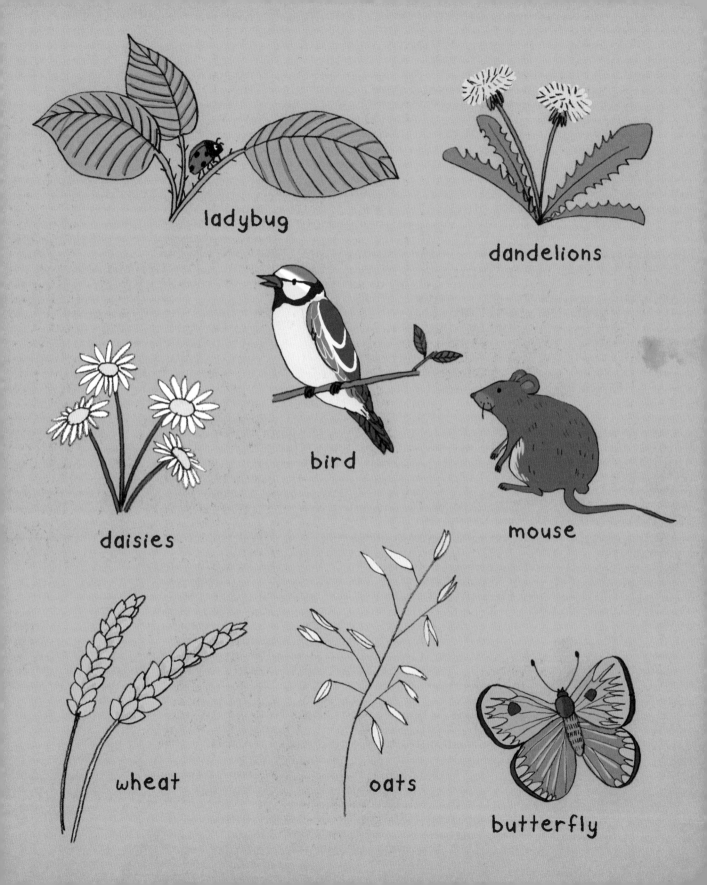

ladybug

dandelions

daisies

bird

mouse

wheat

oats

butterfly

"Welcome to the farm!"

henhouse

rabbit hutch

duck pond

shed

beehives

pigpen

barn

orchard

fields

Feeding the ducks

duck ducklings drake

dragonfly toad

tadpole water lilies

fish

Playing with the chickens

hen

rooster

chicks

radishes

zucchini

pumpkin

carrots

lettuce

leeks

potatoes

herbs

seeds

gardening tools

rabbit hutch

"So soft!"

barn

manure

Milking the cow

Picking fruit

apple

pear

apricots

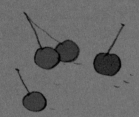

cherries

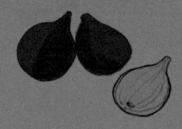

figs

oranges

hazelnuts

peach

plums

jams

pie

juices

donkey

pony

"Look, I'm a cowboy!"

Having a picnic

"Peekaboo!"

hay

beehives

honey

candy

bread

boar

pigpen

sow

piglets

"Yuck!"

Kidding around

shed

sheep

lamb

"Are you looking for your mom?"

tractor

"I'm driving!"

plow

combine

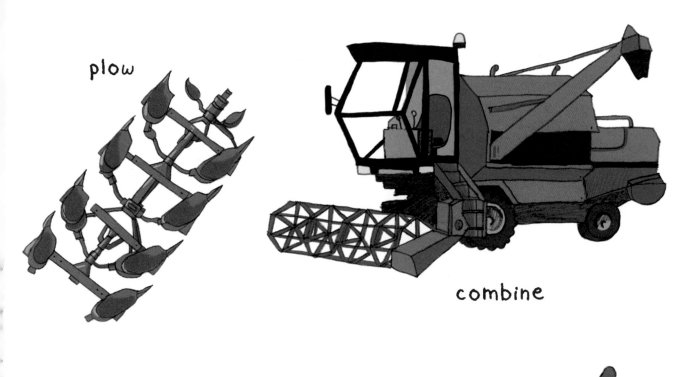

bale of straw

pitchfork

rake

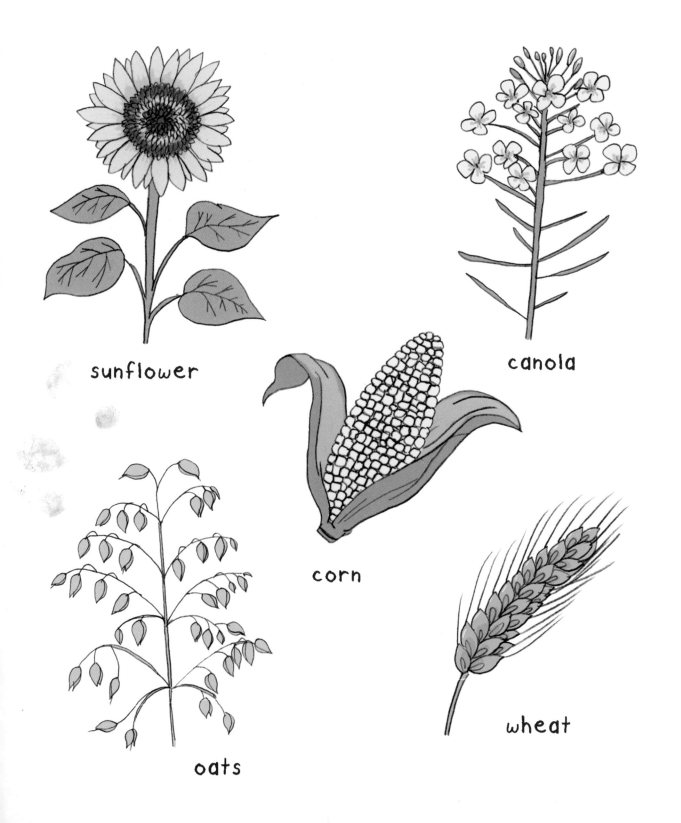

sunflower

canola

corn

oats

wheat

scarecrow

"See you next time!"